Samuel French Acting Edition

The Light

by Loy A. Webb

SAMUELFRENCH.COM SAMUELFRENCH.CO.UK

ISBN 978-0-573-70835-0

www.SamuelFrench.com
www.SamuelFrench.co.uk

MUSIC USE NOTE

IMPORTANT BILLING AND CREDIT REQUIREMENTS

THE LIGHT premiered at MCC Theater's Robert W. Wilson Theater in New York City on February 10, 2019. The production was directed by Logan Vaughn, with set design by Kimie Nishikawa, costume design by Emilio Sosa, lighting design by Ben Stanton, sound design by Elisheba Ittoop, and dramaturgy by Ignacia Delgado. The cast was as follows:

GENESIS.. Mandi Masden
RASHAD.. McKinley Belcher III

THE LIGHT was originally developed at the New Colony (Andrew Hobgood and Evan Linder, Co-Artistic Directors; Stephanie Shum, Managing Director) in Chicago, Illinois. The New Colony presented the world premiere at the Den Theatre in January 2018. The production was directed by Toma Langston, with set design by John Wilson, wardrobe design by Raymond K. Cleveland, lighting design by Cassandra Kendall, sound design by Antonio Bruno, and dramaturgy by Regina Victor. The stage manager was Daryl Ritchie. The cast was as follows:

GENESIS.. Tiffany Oglesby
RASHAD.. Jeffery Owen Freelon Jr.

CHARACTERS

GENESIS – an African-American woman, natural hair, mid-to-late thirties
RASHAD – an African-American man, mid-to-late thirties

SETTING

A Hyde Park condo
Chicago, IL

TIME

October 5, 2018

AUTHOR'S NOTES

1. Genesis and Rashad's song mentioned in the script must be an original jazzy, soulful groove, overflowing with the idealistic love we all dream about. It can just be music, or if a voice is added it must be that of a black woman, with a neo-soul vibe. It should be played three times: at the top of the show, in the middle where it is specified, and at the curtain call.

2. Moments and Pauses mentioned in the script should be extended silences where emotional moments are conveyed without words. All silences should be filled with some unspoken emotion, not just simply silence. Please note, "a moment" is a longer silence than a pause.

3. Please be aware that Genesis and Rashad's banter and jokes, particularly in the beginning, are rooted purely in love and jest. With that said, it should be conveyed that way. It is an opportunity to have fun with these people. Not portray them as having anger or hostility toward each other. This is simply their way of being.

4. Kashif is pronounced "Kuh-Sheef" and Raitima is pronounced "Rah-Team-Uh."

5. Double slash (//) marks indicate where overlapping dialogue begins.

For every black woman or girl that has been through darkness,
I hope this play is the light you have so desperately been praying for.

Scene One

(Genesis's living room. It is sophisticated and cozy. Her walls are adorned with paintings that showcase beautiful, resilient, and strong African-American women. Images that might say they have been through the ringer but made it out alive. Numerous educator awards, African art pieces, and books about both her culture and the world at large are throughout. **RASHAD** *is hiding two envelopes. Their song fills the air.* He takes out a ring box, opens it, and looks at it for a beat. This is a moment after much heartbreak he never thought would come. It's here. He takes a deep, nervous breath to gather himself. He looks at the time.)*

RASHAD. Shit.

(He hurriedly hides the ring and quickly turns off the music. He pretends to clean.)

(A moment.)

*(***GENESIS*** enters.)*

Hey baby. Was trying clean before you got home.

(He clearly doesn't know how to clean to save his life.)

GENESIS. You? Clean?

RASHAD. Yes me. Clean. Can't a man clean for his woman?

---

*A license to produce *The Light* does not include a performance license for any third-party or copyrighted music. Licensees should create an original composition or use music in the public domain. For further information, please see Music Use Note on page 3.

(He clumsily hits some part of his body.)

RASHAD. Ow.

GENESIS. Rashad we've been together how long? And not once have you volunteered to clean. You don't even clean your own house. Mama Joyce does.

RASHAD. Okay and a brotha trying to turn a new leaf. Start fresh for the fall.

GENESIS. It's the first week of October.

RASHAD. It's never too late to become a better man for your woman.

GENESIS. Okay, what did you break?

RASHAD. Don't do that Gen. I'm sitting up here trying to evolve as a man –

GENESIS. Well in that case, whatever it is no.

RASHAD. Amazing. Absolutely amazing. A man tryna show his woman he appreciate // her.

GENESIS. Oh my // god.

RASHAD. Make her load a little lighter after a hard day's // work.

GENESIS. Now I know you // lying.

RASHAD. And you come through the door downing him. See that's the problem with black women. Don't know how to appreciate the black man.

GENESIS. And you know the problem with "the black man"? They don't do what they're asked to do until either – a – they did something wrong, or – b – want something. Which motivated you?

RASHAD. I don't have to put up with this emotional abuse. I know my worth. Clean your own damn house.

GENESIS. You weren't cleaning anyway fool. Been here all day. Then the moment I come home you wanna miraculously clean.

RASHAD. I'm getting tired of you two task masters bossing me around.

GENESIS. Two?

RASHAD. Yes, two. Munch think she a mini you. The other day I come in from my shift at the firehouse. Mind you I'm dog-tired. Only thing I'm thinking about is the bed. I take off my coat, set my bag down, head to my room. When I feel a tap.

GENESIS. A tap?

RASHAD. She point to my wrist talking 'bout some, "Pop-Pop where yo bracelet?"

(He fiddles with a handmade little girl's bracelet on his wrist.)

I say, "It's on my dresser." She say, "I made it to protect you from the fire. Not be on yo dresser. Go get it." I said, "Excuse you?" She put her hands on her hips, rolled her neck, "You heard me." I bent down where we were eye to eye. Put my deep daddy authoritative voice on.

GENESIS. Authoritative voice huh?

RASHAD. You know the one that's the equivalent of that...

(He recreates the face.)

"Boy if you don't sit yo ass down" look.

*(**GENESIS** laughs.)*

GENESIS. You are so silly.

RASHAD. So I gave her that look, but with my James Earl Jones voice. I said, "Do you pay bills in this sucka?" She poke her lil' lip out, looking up at me with them sad puppy dog eyes, "No." I said, "Then you don't get to tell me what to do. I'm your daddy. You not mine. Now watch who you talking to." She run off to my mama crying. Of course Mama babying her. Them tears may phase Mama, but not me. She betta leave that neck rolling and smart mouth where she found it.

GENESIS. Then what you do?

RASHAD. It's my house. A house I bought and paid for. What-chu think I did?

GENESIS. Put it on.

RASHAD. You see it ain't left my wrist.

GENESIS. I taught my ladybug well.

RASHAD. She five going on fifty-five Gen. Seems like yesterday her mama left her on my doorstep. She looking up at me with them big almond brown eyes like, "Who the heck is you?" And I'm looking at her with the same expression like, "Nah lil' girl who the heck is you?" Us both trying to figure out what we gon' do with each other. Four years later she talkin' about some, "You heard me." Ain't that something?

GENESIS. Leave Amaya alone.

RASHAD. I'mma leave her alone alright. Next month's bills going right in her hands.

GENESIS. You love it.

RASHAD. I do. She never ceases to amaze me. She smarter than a whip. Can tell you about any dinosaur ever existed. Know all her states and presidents. Say you taught her all that. Say y'all go over facts when I'm at work. And I thank you baby. Hell, only president I know is Barack Obama and that's for obvious reasons.

GENESIS. Why are you this way?

RASHAD. You've been a tremendous blessing in both our lives baby. 'Specially mine. It used to get me down thinking about all the failed relationships I had before you.

But I realized that wasn't nothing but life pruning me. Just as it would a tree. Cutting out all the old, damaged and diseased branches that didn't belong. Making room for the one that did...you.

(**GENESIS** *bursts into laughter.*)

Really? I'm trying to have a serious moment and you laugh?

GENESIS. This is so suspect Shad. You were one Drake lyric away from singing.

RASHAD. So a brotha pouring his heart out makes him Drake?

GENESIS. You only do that when you're reflecting on your college football glory days.

RASHAD. See this is exactly why brothas don't share they feelings. 'Cause the moment we do, y'all don't take us serious.

GENESIS. Stop being dramatic.

(**RASHAD** *goes to the kitchen, gets a wine glass and a bottle of wine. He pours a glass.)*

RASHAD. See even though you curse me, I'mma bless you. Here.

GENESIS. Mm-mm, not tonight.

RASHAD. Come on, it's Friday.

GENESIS. I know, but wine ain't gonna cut it. I'mma need prayer and an altar.

RASHAD. Oh gosh, what's wrong? Sit here.

(He pats his lap. She sits.)

GENESIS. Today was a mess. Before I could even get in the door good, I was swarmed by teachers.

RASHAD. Why? What happened?

GENESIS. You know Cindy the new teacher I was telling you about?

RASHAD. The white one?

GENESIS. Yes, Rashad, the white one.

(He laughs.)

Anyway, yesterday she posted this pic on her Instagram that said, "I Stand With Brett." And in the caption she went on and on about how this whole thing was a liberal witch hunt designed to destroy Kavanaugh and the conservatives. And she said something like Dr. Ford is a puppet willingly falling on her own sword for their political agenda...something...something. I don't know.

RASHAD. I'm assuming the teachers found out?

GENESIS. Yeah. One of them took a screenshot of the post. Sent it around. And they all came to my office in an uproar demanding I fire her.

RASHAD. I mean I don't think they're wrong.

GENESIS. In regards to the uproar, no. But firing her, it's not justified.

RASHAD. Mmm, I don't know.

GENESIS. She didn't post during school hours, use school equipment, or break any other rules. I can't fire her for having an alternative view.

RASHAD. A dangerous alternative view. She's essentially saying, regardless of Ford's credible testimony, she doesn't believe her. And that makes me think, what if one of her students comes to her with a story like Ford's. Thinking as their teacher she'd be their safe haven. Will she dismiss them too? As a teacher, especially teaching at an all-black charter school, it's her job to be mentally aligned with what's good for the students and their community. And that shit she talking ain't it.

GENESIS. I hear you. And on a personal level, trust me I am severely disappointed. I liked her. I mean, I do like her. She's one of my best teachers. My students have made tremendous strides under her leadership. But... I don't know. I don't know. When you add all these personal feelings it's complicated, but as principal it's my duty to uphold policy. And under policy, I cannot fire her.

RASHAD. ...

GENESIS. What?

RASHAD. I didn't say anything.

GENESIS. But I feel like you have more to say.

RASHAD. Nope, your duty is to uphold policy.

GENESIS. Now I feel like you're judging me.

RASHAD. You the principal baby. You ain't new to this. You won all type of awards because your students and teachers love you. So whatever decision you make, hey, I rock with it.

GENESIS. Okay, glad you understand.

RASHAD. Hm-huh.

(Pause.)

GENESIS. So what are we doing tonight?

RASHAD. Tonight? What's tonight?

GENESIS. Rashad don't play with me.

RASHAD. I'm serious, what's tonight? You gon' take me off punishment and finally give me some booty?

GENESIS. ...

RASHAD. Why you looking at me like that? Oh damn. Is it your birthday? My bad baby. What you wanna do?

GENESIS. You know it's not my birthday fool.

RASHAD. It's not? Then what is it?

GENESIS. I shouldn't have to remind you.

RASHAD. Ah don't be like that Gen.

(He tries to kiss her. She moves her face out the way.)

So you not gon' tell me?

GENESIS. ...

RASHAD. Mannnn if looks could kill, I'll be dead.

GENESIS. ...

RASHAD. You got a booger in your nose.

GENESIS. Goodbye Rashad. And don't come back here until you –

RASHAD. What? Remember our anniversary?

GENESIS. Why do you insist on playing with me?

RASHAD. Because it's funny.

GENESIS. Ugh. You get on my last nerve. Where's my gift?

RASHAD. Your gift?

GENESIS. Yes. I won't believe you actually remembered until I see some gifts. You are not to be trusted.

RASHAD. Naw, you ain't to be trusted. Where's my gift? It's my anniversary too.

GENESIS. Oh I have a gift. Two in fact. Because I actually remembered.

RASHAD. Show me.

GENESIS. Same time.

RASHAD. Ain't no same time. I want to see my gift so I know it's real.

GENESIS. Don't use a me on me.

RASHAD. Show me my gift dammit.

GENESIS. Did you buy me a gift Rashad?

RASHAD. Yes, I told you already.

GENESIS. Then why can't you go first?

RASHAD. Mines is better.

GENESIS. I doubt it.

RASHAD. Just show me the gift woman 'fore I take mines and leave.

GENESIS. Fine.

(She exits. **RASHAD** *quickly grabs the things he hid earlier and puts them in his pockets. He is clearly nervous.* **GENESIS** *re-enters.)*

Did you really remember today was our anniversary?

RASHAD. How many times we gon' go through this? Yes.

GENESIS. Gift one.

(She tries to hand it to him. He reaches for it, but she snatches it away.)

I know you think I hate football. Which I do. It's sexist. Misogynistic. The players have no necks and look like slow idiots running into other grown-ass men // for fun.

RASHAD. I get it baby. I get // it.

GENESIS. I said all that to say, regardless of my personal feelings, I know you love it and would give anything to be on that field. And while I cannot give you your dream back, I can give you a season pass to watch your favs...the Bears.

(She hands him the gift.)

RASHAD. Aww baby, you ain't have to do that.

GENESIS. No you work hard and deserve that time to enjoy yourself, without being stuck up under me and Munch all day.

RASHAD. Now gift two.

GENESIS. Unh-unh ain't no gift two.

RASHAD. Where's my gift two woman?

GENESIS. It's hidden somewhere in this house, and it's gonna stay hidden until I see my gift.

RASHAD. Give me twenty minutes. It's at the Dollar Tree.

GENESIS. You know what...

RASHAD. I'm joking baby. Calm down. Damn. You remember how we met?

GENESIS. Boy do I remember.

RASHAD. I was standing outside the school, minding my business, tending to my daughter. I look over.

Just a quick glance over and I see this chick foaming at the mouth over my ripped and tight body.

GENESIS. I'm sorry your ripped and tight what?

RASHAD. Don't play me Genesis. I might not be there now, 'cause you be cooking all this good food as a ploy to ruin my body // so I won't be attractive to other women.

GENESIS. Oh my God.

RASHAD. But make no mistake when you met me I was ripped and tight.

(He makes some gesture to indicate he was ripped and tight.)

GENESIS. The only thing *ripped and tight* on you was them distressed skinny jeans // you had on sir.

RASHAD. First of all, first of all, let's make something clear. I don't wear skinny jeans. Nor have I ever *bought* or *owned* a pair of skinny jeans.

GENESIS. That's not what your legs were saying boo boo when they was trying to escape from them tight-ass jeans.

RASHAD. If you cared to know the truth, you would know my moms washed my clothes that day, they shrunk, and I grabbed the first thing I saw rushing out the house.

GENESIS. If you say so.

RASHAD. Don't turn this on me. We were talking about you and your morally corrupt ways.

GENESIS. Morally corrupt?

RASHAD. Call yourself somebody principal and you bending all down seductively in front of me. Acting like you was trying to talk to Munch. Looking back making sure I could see the view like Loretta Devine in *Waiting to Exhale*. I peeped you girl. I peeped you.

GENESIS. You just told on yourself. I'm sitting up here on the first day of school greeting students. As a principal should. I see a little girl hysterically crying. You had my baby's hair sticking straight up like Alfalfa from the *Little Rascals*. Had her in mix-match socks. I go over to calm her // and –

RASHAD. Or, or...

GENESIS. Or what?

RASHAD. Was that your excuse?

GENESIS. Excuse for what?

RASHAD. Holla at her fine-ass // daddy.

GENESIS. Boy if you don't get cho behind on. I'm trying to calm her, because she thinks starting school for the first time is terrifying. Meanwhile, you're being a perv staring at my ass.

RASHAD. Perv? Wasn't nobody being no perv. I was obeying the law.

GENESIS. The what fool?

RASHAD. The law. You put an ass that big in front of me, it's illegal not to look. And you know what happens to brothas who look like me when we don't obey the law. I'm just trying to stay alive.

GENESIS. Rashad goodbye. Go get my gift.

RASHAD. Stop being a gold digger.

GENESIS. Please. The only gold I want from you, is the one that goes right here.

(She points to her ring finger.)

RASHAD. You talking about the thumb?

GENESIS. You see what finger I'm pointing to fool.

RASHAD. Oh the index.

GENESIS. I know this time next year, this finger better see some gold. Or...

RASHAD. Or what?

GENESIS. You getting the boot.

RASHAD. All we've been through huh?

GENESIS. Shad, stop playing. We already discussed this. Next year. Ring. This finger.

RASHAD. We'll see.

GENESIS. Ain't no we'll see.

RASHAD. I said we'll see. Between now and next year I might want to marry my other lady. She knows how to treat me right.

GENESIS. Please, don't nobody want you. And the only reason I do, is because my biological clock is ticking and I'm desperate.

*(**RASHAD** is not amused. She laughs and tries to hug him.)*

I'm joking baby.

RASHAD. Nah. The tongue speaks what the heart feels.

GENESIS. Stop being sensitive and lets get back on point. My gift.

RASHAD. Our first date. What was it?

GENESIS. Why do you stay trying to deflect from my gift?

RASHAD. Just answer.

GENESIS. We went to see Raitima at the Promontory.

RASHAD. All I remember was walking in the Promontory, smelling nothing but cocoa butter and coconut oil. That's how you know black women in the building when you smell cocoa butter or coconut oil.

GENESIS. You are so silly.

RASHAD. I'm trying to watch the stage but all y'all naturals in there with your twist outs, braids outs and wash-n-gos blocking the view.

GENESIS. Respect the crown.

RASHAD. Oh I respects the crown. Only God himself can create hair that beautiful where it sits closer to him.

(Pause.)

And you remember what happened when she started singing our song?

GENESIS. Yes.

*(**RASHAD** cuts on their song.*)*

RASHAD. We danced like we were the only two in that room. Remember?

GENESIS. Yes.

*(They dance to their song, recreating the moment. Then, at a point in the middle of the song, **RASHAD** brings her back down to Earth by staring in her eyes.)*

(He kisses her deeply and passionately. He turns the music off.)

RASHAD. How long ago was that?

GENESIS. Two years.

RASHAD. Two years. That kiss. Us.

GENESIS. Two years. That kiss. Us.

(She gets excited thinking he is going to propose. Instead, he pulls out an envelope.)

Oh.

(He hands it to her.)

What's this?

(She shakes the envelope.)

RASHAD. What you shaking it for?

GENESIS. Trying to see if it gives me a clue.

RASHAD. Just open it woman.

---

*A license to produce *The Light* does not include a performance license for any third-party or copyrighted music. Licensees should create an original composition or use music in the public domain. For further information, please see Music Use Note on page 3.

GENESIS. Okay, okay.

(She slowly opens the envelope and pulls out a handwritten letter.)

RASHAD. Read it.

(She reads it silently to herself.)

Out loud.

GENESIS. Dear Genesis,

I am a man with a sizable appetite. I'll eat your plate, my plate, then go home and eat some more. My daughter always says, "Pop-Pop, I don't see how all that fits in your belly." I don't either. But it does and I never seem to get full. And you know that confused me until tonight. You see tonight, I realized this entire time I was feeding my body, all the while unconsciously neglecting my soul.

My soul was starving. It was starving for a woman whose magnetic smile could fill all the crevices left in my life by sadness, hurt and disappointment, with joy.

It was starving for a woman whose intelligence could inspire me to pick up more books about politics, history, art, the plight of our people in America and the world at large, just so I could keep up with her brilliance.

It was starving for a woman whose gentle touch could awaken the parts in me that no longer wanted to just survive. But live life with such a sense of vigor, passion, and urgency that went beyond survival to thrive.

And as Raitima's voice echoed throughout the Promontory // I –

RASHAD. I leaned down and kissed you. And it was then I realized this entire time the woman my soul was starving for Genesis...was you.

GENESIS. And if you're reading this now it means that my soul has been full since that day...

RASHAD & GENESIS. And I want your presence to nourish me for my entire life.

RASHAD. What's the postmark date on the envelope?

(She looks.)

GENESIS. October 6, 2016. Wait, you mailed this the day after our first date?

RASHAD. Yup. Which would be...

GENESIS. Tomorrow. Which means you wrote this letter two years ago today?

RASHAD. It only took me one night to know there was nobody I wanted to spend my forever with, besides you.

(He gets on one knee in front of her and pulls out a ring box.)

GENESIS. Oh my God. Oh my God.

RASHAD. I know we said next year, but I've seen all I need to see to know I want you as my wife. Genesis Marie Washington, will you marry me?

GENESIS. You serious?

RASHAD. Nah, I'm joking. Yes I'm serious.

GENESIS. Yes! Yes!

*(**RASHAD** puts the ring on her finger. She is so filled with emotion, she can't speak.)*

RASHAD. You don't have to say anything. Yes is enough. Happy Anniversary baby.

*(**GENESIS** grabs him into an embrace and kisses all over his face excitedly.)*

GENESIS. I love you. I love you. I love you.

(He laughs at her excitement.)

RASHAD. Aight Gen. Love you too. Now...

(He brings her over to the wine.)

Let's toast to you being the future Mrs...

RASHAD & GENESIS. Rashad Tate.

*(**RASHAD** pours a drink. **GENESIS** looks at her ring in awe.)*

GENESIS. Oh it's so beautiful baby. Oh my God.

RASHAD. To us.

GENESIS. Actually baby after doing this, I wanna toast to you.

RASHAD. What for?

GENESIS. Stealing my heart in New Orleans. That trip was one of the best experiences of my life. We both needed a break. There was that sale for round-trip tickets. And... we just went. No plan, nothing. Just went. Thinking back on it, that was absolutely crazy.

RASHAD. Why?

GENESIS. We'd only been dating, what? Three weeks. I didn't know you like that. You could've been crazy.

RASHAD. Excuse you? You went because you couldn't resist my good looks.

GENESIS. I went because I couldn't resist the free trip. // You was offering. I was taking.

RASHAD. Wow. So that's what I was to you? A free trip?

GENESIS. Basically.

RASHAD. Ain't that some shit.

GENESIS. But seriously baby, that trip... Us dancing all night to the jazz bands, as we strolled down Frenchmen Street.

RASHAD. You dragging me every two seconds to Cafe Du Monde for some damn beignets.

GENESIS. Sorry. They were addictive.

RASHAD. Forget them beignets. That food period, was addictive.

GENESIS. Fareal. We should go back to do nothing but eat.

RASHAD. Yes let's make that happen. And this time, I'mma actually get to a Saints game.

GENESIS. Shad, I didn't go on vacation to spend my last day of it at no damn football game.

RASHAD. I wasn't too mad tho.

GENESIS. I know you weren't.

RASHAD. We did the only thing I'll take over football. Unless it's the Super Bowl. Then even *that* can't hold my attention.

GENESIS. Anyway, that was the day I fell for you.

RASHAD. That's what happens when I put that thang on you.

GENESIS. It had absolutely nothing to do with "that thang." Okay.

RASHAD. You sure?

(He makes some playful flirtatious gesture to jog her memory. Pause.)

GENESIS. Well maybe a little.

(Pause.)

Well maybe a lot. But "that thang" ain't the point. The point is, what stole my heart was what you did before that. Since it was raining so hard, we couldn't really go anywhere. We were just laughing, joking, discussing life. You were looking like a snack. I was looking like a snack. We were finally going to do what two snacks do... I immediately went into my routine. Covers on. Lights off. But you Mr. Tate...you softly grabbed my hand, kissed it, and turned the lights back on. And that was scary. You not just looking at me, but actually seeing me. But there was something about you that made me feel secure enough to go against my routine. And I took a deep breath, let the covers go and said here I am. Flaws and all. Then you explored my body with your hands and planted soft butterfly kisses in places no one had ever seen. And with each kiss I felt you were saying, "This flaws-and-all Gen, is the Gen that I want." And I was like, if this is what you want then honey you can have it. How you want it? Want it baked? Want it fried? Want it sautéed? Would you like a side of ten kids, 'cause you can have that too.

RASHAD. Shit, I want *all* that.

(A moment.)

GENESIS. That's when I knew you were the one for me.

RASHAD. You never told me that before.

GENESIS. Well now you know.

(Pause.)

RASHAD. Thank you.

GENESIS. You're welcome.

RASHAD. I think that's deserving of a second anniversary gift. What you think?

GENESIS. Wait? There's more?

RASHAD. I got a little something up my sleeve.

GENESIS. I can't take it. I can't take it.

RASHAD. Now for this surprise I pulled a couple strings with my peoples.

GENESIS. Your peoples?

RASHAD. In high places.

GENESIS. Oooo and who are these peoples?

RASHAD. Don't worry about it. Just know tonight...

(He pulls out another envelope.)

I got us tickets to see Raitima at –

*(**GENESIS** totally freaks out.)*

Damn, you screaming louder for her than the ring.

GENESIS. Sorry baby. I love her. She's my fav. Oh my God, what am I going to wear, my hair is a mess, my nails aren't done. You can't just drop this on me.

(She exits into her bedroom.)

RASHAD. You trying to marry her or me?

GENESIS. *(Offstage.)* Where is it? I wanna know what to wear.

RASHAD. Union Park.

*(**GENESIS** peeks her head out.)*

GENESIS. Union Park?

RASHAD. Yeah she's performing at the "Heal the Chi" concert hosted by Ka–

*(**GENESIS** re-enters.)*

GENESIS. Kashif.

RASHAD. Yeah. Some of everybody gon' be there. Chance, Common, Jamila Woods, BJ the Chicago Kid. It's Kashif's way of bringing the city together through // all this violence.

GENESIS. I know the purpose of the concert.

RASHAD. You hate his music. I know. But he's a small part.

GENESIS. Small part? It's his concert Shad. How is that a small part?

RASHAD. 'Cause it's not about him. It's about bringing the city together in the midst of all this tragedy. Vibing to good music. Eating good food. They gon' have all the Chicago eats there. We gon' be munching on that good Garrett's Popcorn. And guess what else gon' be there.

GENESIS. I don't –

RASHAD. Just guess baby.

GENESIS. What?

RASHAD. A six-piece, mild sauce, fries, salt and pepper, fried hard. Now you know you can't turn down no Harold's Chicken.

GENESIS. While that sounds appetizing, no.

RASHAD. Come on Gen, Raitima is performing and these tickets give us backstage access.

GENESIS. I don't care Shad. If Kashif is there, I don't want to go. Raitima wasn't even on the list of people performing.

RASHAD. I was telling my boy Rodney at the firehouse about our first date and how I was gonna propose. He told me his brother works at the radio station co-hosting the concert and said Raitima is gonna be a surprise guest. He got his brother to give us these as a gift.

GENESIS. And I'm appreciative baby.

RASHAD. But you don't want to go?

GENESIS. No.

RASHAD. Your feelings that strong?

GENESIS. Yes.

RASHAD. One night, you can't put whatever you got against him aside?

GENESIS. Baby listen, I'm not trying to be difficult. But I can't support Kashif. Let's do something else.

RASHAD. I don't want to do anything else Gen.

GENESIS. I don't need anything fancy. A simple dinner will do.

RASHAD. Baby, the average ticket for this event was 100 dollars.

GENESIS. Okay.

RASHAD. Okay and somebody gave us these tickets for free. Not just regular tickets, but VIP tickets, which run between 300 and 500 dollars.

GENESIS. And I will give you every dime back.

RASHAD. I don't want the money Gen. I want the memories. On our engagement night. Us grooving to Raitima. Me holding you close. Us laughing and joking about old times. Us plotting new ones.

GENESIS. Baby I know that would be beautiful. I know. But I can't. How about we call Rodney and see if his brother can give the tickets to somebody else while we figure out what to do?

RASHAD. That's gon' make me look bad Gen. He already pulled hella strings.

GENESIS. Not if we say an emergency came up. People understand things happen.

RASHAD. Baby, baby, baby, baby. Let me see if I can explain this to you. We both know I ain't no planner // but I took the time to plan this engagement thoroughly, because I wanted to make it perfect for you.

GENESIS. Unh-unh.

And it is perfect.

RASHAD. And Gen, I ain't just start planning yesterday. I planned six months in advance. Back then I started working overtime. Twenty-four-hour shifts back to back. Just to afford you that...that...that...

GENESIS. Why you making a face like you constipated?

RASHAD. 'Cause I hurt every time I think about how I spent *ten, thousand, dollars*, on that ring you rocking.

GENESIS. You did not have to spend that Rashad.

RASHAD. Yes I did 'cause we all know how women get if the ring ain't right.

GENESIS. Baby, it's the thought not the price.

RASHAD. You say it's the thought not the price. Then if the ring ain't right, you'd be dogging me to your friends. "Gurllll, this nigga got me fucked up trying to propose with this Cracker Jack box ass ring."

GENESIS. First off, I don't talk like that.

RASHAD. Not all the time. But every now and again, that Englewood creeps up out cha. And I wasn't trying to deal with 73rd and Peoria Genesis. You ain't always had a condo in Hyde Park now. And you couldn't be a Chatham boy like me.

GENESIS. Yeah, yeah.

RASHAD.	**GENESIS.**
So with that said, I did what I needed to do, to get you that beautiful ring you rocking. // Then because I love and respect you so much, I went to your parents to get their blessing. And you already know who gave me a hard time.	It is beautiful.

GENESIS. Daddy.

RASHAD. Exactly, but I wasn't going to make this move without yo mama and Forest Whitaker's approval. You know I get scared when he stare at me with that dead eye.

GENESIS. Don't do my daddy stupid.

RASHAD. And on top of that Rodney came through for us because these tickets were sold out.

GENESIS. I'm not taking any of this for granted baby. Trust me.

RASHAD. Gen and the sad part about all this, is I almost died during this process.

GENESIS. Died?

RASHAD. Yes died. I don't know if you know this, but I got a weak heart. And this whole thing practically sent me into cardiac arrest. Wondering was I making the right decision? Would this be perfect? Would you say no? The pearly gates were calling Gen. They were calling.

GENESIS. Rashad, I appreciate every bit of effort you put into today. This is literally one of the best days of my life. But I can't go. I just can't.

RASHAD. Come on Gen, why?

GENESIS. I told you already, his music is disrespectful to women and I don't want to spend my special night around him or that toxicity.

RASHAD. Why do you keep saying that?

GENESIS. Saying what?

RASHAD. His music is disrespectful to women. He speaks on police brutality, racism, poverty, a fucked up government. It's all positive.

GENESIS. Positive in regards to black men. Any time he mentions women it's something negative. Warning men to stay away from us, because we want to use them, trap them, ruin them, or can't take care of our kids.

RASHAD. And Beyoncé, Mary J. Blige, and Keyshia Cole don't make songs about how no good men are?

GENESIS. It's not the same.

RASHAD. Why? 'Cause they in yo rotation?

GENESIS. No, because it's the truth. Half y'all ain't no good.

RASHAD. Oh, but when Sheef tell our side he wrong?

GENESIS. Everything that comes out his mouth in regards to women is a stereotype. We're either gold-digging hoes or no-good baby mamas. How is that positive?

RASHAD. Baby, while you're not like that. Thank God. It's a lot of trifling women out here. Case and point Munch's mama.

GENESIS. That was an isolated incident.

RASHAD. Hm. So it's an isolated incident to // date me even though she had a whole-ass husband.

GENESIS. Here we go.

RASHAD. I break up with her because I have enough respect for myself to not be somebody's fucking side piece. A year later she pop up on my doorstep talking about I got a daughter. And oh no. Having a surprise daughter isn't enough. She tells me her husband's job is leaving, and he said if they wanna stay married, she gotta leave Munch here. So what does she do? She leaves my daughter on a doorstep Genesis. Doorstep. She ain't called this little girl in over four years, or sent her enough money to buy a damn sandwich. And you telling me that's an isolated incident?

GENESIS. It is.

RASHAD. Is it an isolated incident for women, or is that how men "supposedly" are?

(She is annoyed and silent.)

Ahh see Gen, you bias. Things like that ain't no isolated incident. More brothas go through trifling shit with women than y'all care to admit. It's just nobody is brave or vulnerable enough beside Sheef to talk about it for fear of looking soft. And if it's okay for y'all to listen to Beyoncé out here, "Middle fingers up tell 'em boy bye." I don't see the problem with me listening to Sheef tell my truth.

GENESIS. Wait you listen to his music?

RASHAD. Huh?

GENESIS. You heard me.

RASHAD. I do. Sometimes.

GENESIS. I asked you not to play his music.

RASHAD. And I don't. Around you.

GENESIS. I meant period.

RASHAD. I'm not some little boy Gen. You can't tell me what I can and cannot listen to.

(She gets his cell phone and scrolls through.)

What are you doing?

GENESIS. You literally have all four of his albums on your phone.

RASHAD. How is it hurting you on my phone? You told me you didn't like his music, I never played it around you again. But what I listen to by myself is my business.

GENESIS. It's about respecting my wishes Rashad.

(She puts his phone down in a huff.)

RASHAD. Baby sit next to me.

GENESIS. No.

RASHAD. Please.

GENESIS. No Rashad.

RASHAD. Pretty please.

GENESIS. What?

RASHAD. Just sit.

(She sits away from him. He goes over to her.)

Put your feet right here.

(He pats his lap.)

GENESIS. Nope.

RASHAD. Why?

GENESIS. 'Cause it's not gonna work this time.

RASHAD. What's not gon' work?

GENESIS. Don't play stupid. You know what you do.

RASHAD. What do I do?

(He grabs one of her feet and begins to massage it.)

GENESIS. You think you slick.

RASHAD. No, I'm just trying to relax you.

GENESIS. You not getting the other one. Nope.

RASHAD. You sure?

(She starts to really feel the massage.)

GENESIS. Ugh, I hate you.

(She puts her other foot up. He massages both.)

RASHAD. I knew you would let me massage these bear claws.

GENESIS. Whatever. Just know I'm still mad fool.

RASHAD. Okay.

GENESIS. Ain't no okay. I'm serious Rashad. This is not done.

RASHAD. I hear you. But can you explain what's your deal with Sheef? I mean you don't like his music. I kinda get that. But is it something else? I don't see what's the big deal about the concert. We would be going for us, not him.

GENESIS. He's a hypocrite Rashad.

RASHAD. Hypocrite?

GENESIS. Yes and I refuse to support someone who doesn't live what they preach.

RASHAD. How is he a hypocrite?

GENESIS. His whole "conscious" persona is a facade.

(He laughs.)

RASHAD. You cannot be serious?

GENESIS. Yes. I'm very serious actually.

RASHAD. Gen if there's anybody that's a righteous brotha it's Sheef.

GENESIS. Well I know him, and I'm telling you he's not.

RASHAD. Wait, you know him?

GENESIS. Yes.

RASHAD. Why did you never tell me this?

GENESIS. I didn't think it was relevant.

RASHAD. So y'all dated?

GENESIS. No, we went to undergrad together.

RASHAD. But baby that was almost what? Seventeen, eighteen years ago? I'm sure he's matured since then.

GENESIS. I highly doubt it.

RASHAD. You doubt it? Baby, Sheef loves our people, especially the black people in this city.

GENESIS. And what does that mean?

RASHAD. What do you mean what does that mean?

GENESIS. Just because the message is righteous, doesn't mean the messenger is.

RASHAD. Everything he speaks about in his music, aligns with his life. Everything.

GENESIS. You only know him through his music.

RASHAD. And you sure y'all ain't date?

GENESIS. No we did not. Why do you keep asking me that?

RASHAD. Because usually when women go this hard on a dude, its over a relationship gone wrong and you're sounding a wee bit like a bitter ex.

GENESIS. Wow.

(Pause.)

RASHAD. That came out wrong.

GENESIS. Did it? Because that seemed very intentional to me.

RASHAD. Listen baby, all I'm saying is –

GENESIS. Don't touch me.

(Silence.)

RASHAD. If you dated him I don't // care. I'm not tripping off the past.

GENESIS. We did not date. I already told you.

RASHAD. Then did he do something to you?

GENESIS. No.

RASHAD. Then what could you possibly have against this man?

GENESIS. He's a rapist Rashad.

(Pause.)

Does that...clarify enough about your "righteous" brotha?

RASHAD. A what?

GENESIS. You heard me. Now do you see why I was so adamant about not going? How is he gonna be some "brother do good," but he's out here raping women. You can't do "good" for the black community, yet hurt the women who reside in that community. That's not freedom fighting, that's comedy. It's a fucking joke.

RASHAD. How do you know he raped someone?

GENESIS. She was my friend. We worked at the campus library together.

RASHAD. And Kashif raped her?

GENESIS. Yes.

(Pause.)

RASHAD. He ever arrested or...

GENESIS. No.

RASHAD. And you know this for sure. That he...

GENESIS. Yes, while we were in college.

(Pause.)

RASHAD. Why was he never arrested?

GENESIS. What?

RASHAD. You said he did this to your friend. But he wasn't arrested. Why?

GENESIS. She never came forward.

RASHAD. Then how do you know for sure?

GENESIS. She told me.

RASHAD. So he was never disciplined by the school?

GENESIS. No.

RASHAD. And he never admitted to it?

GENESIS. Why do you keep asking all these questions?

RASHAD. These questions are important Gen. Trying to get a picture of the whole story.

GENESIS. The whole story is that he raped her. The end.

RASHAD. I don't know. That doesn't seem like something he'd do.

GENESIS. Excuse me? Are you defending a rapist?

RASHAD. I'm not defending anybody. I'm saying it doesn't seem like his character. He's more vocal than anybody about the violence in the city.

GENESIS. Okay.

RASHAD. He uses millions of his own money to buy textbooks for schools in the hood –

GENESIS. Okay.

RASHAD. – Create summer jobs to keep kids off the street.

GENESIS. Okay.

RASHAD. He's opened shelters for single mothers all over Chicago.

GENESIS. You can do all those things and still be a rapist.

RASHAD. I think we should give him the benefit of the doubt.

GENESIS. Benefit of the...? Weren't you against my teacher standing with Kavanaugh, now you're standing with Kashif?

RASHAD. I'm not just standing with Kashif. I'm saying his situation is a bit different.

GENESIS. How? They're both guilty.

RASHAD. See, we have to be careful –

GENESIS. Careful about what?

RASHAD. Let me finish. We have to be careful about prematurely accusing black men before getting all the facts –

GENESIS. My friend telling me Kashif raped her is all the facts you need.

RASHAD. Can I finish or...

GENESIS. No, because you're sounding like a dumbass hotep.

RASHAD. Really? Kavanaugh can get accused of something like this, and go on about his life unscathed. With Kashif, everything he's built will burn down.

GENESIS. Who cares? He raped someone, burn that shit down.

RASHAD. If he actually raped someone, but we need to be sure.

GENESIS. That can't happen when you automatically take Kashif's side.

RASHAD. I didn't do that.

GENESIS. You did. Before I could even get it out, you came for me like the goddamn police.

RASHAD. You told me he raped your friend. And I said okay, let me try to see Kashif's side before jumping to conclusions.

GENESIS. You're really showing your privilege right now.

RASHAD. What Privilege? Black men have the highest rates of imprisonment, dropout rates, // most likelihood of dying a violent death.

GENESIS. That doesn't mean you don't have privilege in relation to black women.

RASHAD. You can't have privilege when you're at the bottom of virtually everything in society.

GENESIS. Actually, black women are at the bottom of virtually everything in society.

RASHAD. See you're making this about black men vs. black women –

GENESIS. No Rashad, I'm calling out your privilege. I told you Kashif raped my friend. You're re-centering the conversation around Kashif and black men. That's black male privilege.

RASHAD. No, I'm thinking about the ramifications for black men –

GENESIS. Again the black man is the focus.

RASHAD. That is what I am.

GENESIS. And the world is bigger than the black man Rashad.

RASHAD. And the bigger world does not include us.

GENESIS. It doesn't include us either. That's what I'm trying to get you to see. We deal with same racist shit y'all do.

RASHAD. It's just a unique struggle for black men.

GENESIS. Really? Because along with being black, black women have to struggle with the complications that come with being a woman. That's unique.

RASHAD. Our whole lives can be yanked from us with one false allegation. No one else goes through that.

GENESIS. You keep talking about these false allegations. Let me make this clear. For rape, which is what we're talking about, that percentage is super small.

RASHAD. And in that percentage, however small, are innocent men.

GENESIS. You frustrating me now. Because you keep zoning in on that fucking small percent.

There is a much larger percentage of women, particularly black women, whose lives have been ravaged by the men that rape them. There's either no accountability or y'all get a slap on the wrist.

RASHAD. But what men are we talking about Genesis? Are we talking about the Kavanaughs of the world or the brothas that look like me? Because the only people I know that get a slap on the wrist are the Kavanaughs.

GENESIS. That's not true.

RASHAD. What are you talking about that's not true? The men who look like me always pay a hefty price.

GENESIS. Oh, I see. It's coming together now. You made this whole hoopla about Ford and her credibility. But not because you believed her. You actually could care less about her credibility. You aligned yourself with her, because she's against what you're against. Which is Kavanaugh and what he symbolizes. The rich white privileged men, that get away with things you never could.

RASHAD. I never said that.

GENESIS. You didn't have to. It's implied. You keep talking about black man this black man that, but you're ignoring black women. Women are never believed. It takes thousands of us coming out of the woodwork for people to finally say, "You know what? She might be telling the truth."

RASHAD. It didn't take a thousand for me. Just one. One who was mad I broke up with her. Then all of sudden the police coming to my apartment arresting me for

domestic battery. It took three years to clear my name. Three years.
And by that time I had lost my scholarship, no other schools wanted to touch me, and my eligibility to play had expired. So I ended up back here as a failure.

GENESIS. She was wrong to lie on you.

RASHAD. Nothing was more embarrassing than having to come back to Chicago with my hat in my hand, having to tell my mother what happened. Folks laughing at me. Shaking they head. "All his mama used to do was brag about him. Now look at him. Nigga blew it. A failure."

GENESIS. You're not a failure, Rashad.

RASHAD. From first playing football when I was five in Pop Warner till college, me and Mama would talk about everything I was going to do for her. Pay her way back through medical school so she could be that doctor she gave up for me when my daddy died. I see it in her eyes sometimes when she look at me. The disappointment. She thinking of what life could've been if only...

GENESIS. You bounced back baby. Got your degree. Bought a house for you, your mom and Munch. And on top of that, you are a young black firefighter. That's like spotting a unicorn in this city. That in itself is an achievement.

RASHAD. That ain't no honor. The racist shit I have to put up with at work.

GENESIS. Okay let them stay mad they threw every hurdle your way, and you still came out on top.

RASHAD. I just feel like life should be different you know?

GENESIS. If life were different, there would be no us. You'd probably be off in the NFL somewhere, having all-white-girl yacht parties like Kyrie Irving.

RASHAD. Kyrie plays basketball baby.

GENESIS. Whatever. All y'all athletes the same.

RASHAD. This one ain't. I would've been focused on winning a Super Bowl, Munch, my mother and you.

GENESIS. While that's an awesome dream to have, just know I am perfectly happy with my ripped and tight firefighter.

RASHAD. You finally admit it.

GENESIS. What?

RASHAD. I was ripped and tight.

GENESIS. Just a dab. Little bitty dab. In the chest area.

RASHAD. Come here.

(He pats his lap. She sits.)

(A moment.)

GENESIS. Sooooo, what do you want to do tonight?

RASHAD. Uh...

GENESIS. Uh what?

RASHAD. I think we should still go to the concert.

GENESIS. Did you not hear anything I just said?

RASHAD. If Kashif did this like you said, we can't let him have power over us. We're not going for him. We're going to celebrate me and you. Two years. That kiss. Us.

GENESIS. Rashad going period is saying we support a rapist.

RASHAD. No it doesn't. If this was an election and he was running for mayor. Then sure. Let's boycott. Let's fight the power. Call Jesse Jackson and Al Sharpton. We don't want a rapist as mayor. But this is just a concert Gen. It ain't worth marching over baby. Chill.

(Pause.)

GENESIS. Oh?

RASHAD. Here we go.

GENESIS. He held my friend down and penetrated her while she screamed stop until her voice and body gave out. That's not worth marching over?

(Pause.)

Answer my question.

RASHAD. Genesis, just forget the concert.

GENESIS. Why can't you see it's bigger than the fucking concert?

RASHAD. What am I not seeing?

GENESIS. By going to the concert, we are failing my friend. It's more than music, it's more than a good time. It's an act of support that is as strong as a vote.

RASHAD. And I said we do not have to go.

GENESIS. You're still not getting my point. Okay maybe this will be clearer. What if it was Munch he did that to?

RASHAD. Don't go there.

GENESIS. No. Answer me. What if it was Munch?

RASHAD. Don't bring my daughter into this.

GENESIS. Oh, I see. Struck a nerve.

RASHAD. I'mma go. You tripping.

(He goes to get his things to leave. **GENESIS** *tries to stop him.)*

GENESIS. No stay and answer me.

RASHAD. Gen move.

GENESIS. No answer me. What if it was Munch he penetrated // until her body gave out?

RASHAD. Stop talking about my fucking daughter! That shit wouldn't happen, because if a muthafucka tried he'd be dead. Move!

GENESIS. But my friend doesn't matter because she isn't your daughter?

RASHAD. I'm out.

(Silence.)

(He grabs his things and heads for the door.)

GENESIS. It was me.

RASHAD. Wait, he did that to you?

(Silence.)

Did he do that to you?

GENESIS. Get out.

(She pushes him toward the door.)

RASHAD. No, please answer my question.

GENESIS. I said get out!

(She now starts to push him more aggressively toward the door.)

RASHAD. Answer me Genesis.

(She pushes him even more aggressively toward the door.)

I said answer me!

(He grabs her hands to stop. She rips them away from his grasp.)

Did he do that to you?

(Silence.)

GENESIS. Please just go.

RASHAD. Not until you answer my question. I need to know whether he did that to you.

GENESIS. Why? So you don't have to feel guilty about all his albums you bump when I'm not around? So you don't have to feel guilty about how you sat up here and defended him like you were defending the Constitution? No. I'm not gonna tell you anything different to clear your conscience. I want you to sit with that. Sit with every word. Every. Fucking. Word you just said to me.

(Silence.)

RASHAD. I asked you earlier did he do something to you and you said no. Why did you lie? Did you know this wouldn't have even been an issue?

GENESIS. Ah see. All you men are the same. The fucking same. See if I didn't have a father, son or man, I would care about black men who die in the street. Like Trayvon, like Eric, like Laquan shot sixteen times right here in this city. I care because they are human. Because their lives did not deserve to be taken. But for us, ah naw the issues don't matter unless it's your "girl, daughter or mother." Being humans worthy of compassion is not enough.

RASHAD. Baby I am sorry. I am tearing up these fucking tickets.

(He tears the tickets.)

GENESIS. I don't care. You said exactly what you meant. I'm not worth marching over. We black girls and women never really are. We are always told that men, little black girl, are more important than your protection. This is exactly why I didn't tell the police. I'm sure they would have told me the same thing. You Genesis Marie Washington aren't worth marching over.

(Silence.)

RASHAD. Baby I am sorry. I am sorry. A million times I am sorry. I –

(Exhausted, **GENESIS** *exits to the bedroom and closes the door.)*

Baby. Baby. Bab–

(He stands alone, exhausted. Unsure of what to do next.)

(He goes to bedroom door. It's locked.)

Baby please come out here and talk to me.

(No answer.)

Baby listen, I know you're upset with me but nothing will get solved by you shutting me out. We have to talk about this.

(No response.)

Gen just...just open the door baby.

(No response.)

Fine. You win. I'mma go. But I'm coming back later and we figuring this out.

(He gets his things to leave.)

(He reaches the door. A moment.)

(He decides against it and makes the conscious decision to stay and fight for his relationship.)

(He stands waiting for her, however long it takes for her to open the door.)

(After about a minute, **GENESIS** *enters.)*

Gen, I messed up.

GENESIS. Why don't you leave already?! I need you to leave.

RASHAD. When you love someone you don't leave. You stay, however long it takes to figure it out. Otherwise relationships fail. And we cannot let us fail Genesis.

GENESIS. Oh so now you're a relationship expert?

RASHAD. No Gen, I'm just admitting that I'm wrong.

GENESIS. And now you can go.

RASHAD. What can I do to make this better?

GENESIS. You really wanna know?

RASHAD. Yes, I really wanna know.

GENESIS. Open the door.

RASHAD. Genesis.

GENESIS. No this will help. I promise.

*(***RASHAD*** reluctantly opens the door.)*

Now stand on the other side.

(She waits for him to stand on the other side. He doesn't.)

I'm waiting for you to stand on the other side so I can tell you how to fix this.

RASHAD. I know what you're gonna say. So no. Genesis, some of us learn the hard way. Sometimes saying the stove is hot ain't enough. Some of us gotta feel the heat against our skin to learn not to touch it again. Teachable moments. That's what they're called. That's what I needed. And I need you to continue to teach me to –

GENESIS. I'm not wasting time on any more men who need teachable moments. It is not my job to teach you! That's the problem. The burden is always on the woman to *teach*. Always carrying, always hauling, always educating men who don't care to learn anyway. Because you know what? After you take them back, they make the same fucking mistakes. I'm too old for this shit. We're not in our twenties or teenagers. I want somebody who gets it. Somebody who already knows. Somebody I don't have to *teach*. Education is my profession. I don't want to do it at home.

RASHAD. And you know that man you get that already knows, somebody taught him. He learned because he dropped the ball maybe ten, twenty times before you. And finally, on woman twenty-one he makes the better decision. Because those other women *taught* him.

GENESIS. Don't you see that as a problem? Why do women have to always be your fucking casualties to getting it?

RASHAD. I don't know. I have to figure it out.

GENESIS. Well figure it out, then find woman twenty-one and treat her better. Goodbye.

RASHAD. Gen just –

GENESIS. Goodbye Rashad.

RASHAD. Gen don't give up on me. I will do whatever it takes to do better.

GENESIS. Goodbye Rashad.

(A moment.)

RASHAD. Okay Gen...okay just...

(Out of desperation, he finds a reason to stay.)

You said you hid a second gift for me.

GENESIS. There's no second gift.

RASHAD. Please.

GENESIS. I said there is no second gift.

RASHAD. Where is it?

(He looks around for it.)

GENESIS. Why won't you just leave?

*(**RASHAD** finds a gift box. She tries to snatch it from him.)*

Give it here.

(They go back and forth over it. Gift paper and a baby onesie fall out. **RASHAD** *picks up the onesie and reads it.)*

RASHAD. "Daddy's First-Round Draft Pick."

*(***GENESIS** *is silent. He looks at her, knowing what this means.)*

(Silence.)

Baby whatever it takes we'll figure it out.

GENESIS. Rashad, please.

RASHAD. Gen I will make sure I'm every bit of the man // you need me to be before we walk down that aisle.

GENESIS. I can't even think about us right now.

(A moment.)

RASHAD. ...Okay. But know whatever you need for our baby I'm there. Appointments, classes, whatever it is.

(Silence.)

You heard me Gen? Whatever you need, just tell me.

GENESIS. Rashad, it's too much... I don't know.

RASHAD. What don't you know?

*(***GENESIS** *is silent.)*

What don't you know?

GENESIS. It's a lot going on right now and I just... A child...? I don't know.

(She is silent.)

RASHAD. You ain't thinking about...? Gen this argument is between me and you. Ain't got nothing to do with our...

*(***GENESIS** *is silent.)*

Genesis.

(A moment.)

Genesis.

GENESIS. I am scared to death to bring a child into this world. What if what happened to me happens to them?

I fought. I fought so hard. I yelled at the top of my lungs for help, and nobody came. His roommates in the other room. I know they heard me. Nobody came. Nobody bust the door down to see what was wrong. Didn't even knock. Just turned the TV up. Turned the fucking TV up. And after that, I just went numb. Couldn't fight anymore. Couldn't yell. Just numb.

I went home, took a bath. Scrubbed myself as hard as I could to get clean. The night played like a broken record in my head. Why did I let him do this? Why didn't I continue to fight? So many whys. And at that moment, I felt life under the water, would be better than above it. But I couldn't do it.

The first person that popped in my head, was my dean. This powerful black woman. She was who I wanted to be. Her office was filled with photos of her and these iconic black women. Her and Bell Hooks. Her and Shirley Chisholm. If anybody was gonna have my back it was her.

And when I told her, you know what she said, "There's only a few of us at this college. Don't ruin your life or his, by airing dirty laundry to these white folks. You're a strong woman, you'll get through it. Let karma repay him."

And ever since then, I never said anything. I waited patiently, and patiently for karma to come and do to him what he did to me. Every day, I said karma gon' come Gen. It's gon' come. You don't have to do nothing. It's gon' come.

But it never did. In fact, I think karma reached his door, and heard him speak about community, quote Du Bois and Malcolm. Heard him spit a hot sixteen. And karma forgot the mission it was on, and fell in love like everybody else.

Karma said fuck Gen. I'mma give him platinum albums. A key to the city. The respect of the people. Arenas full of people screaming his name.

And at this point, karma can stay where it's at. I gave up on that a long time ago. I just need... I just need some light. Just a little bit of light in all this darkness. I am tired. Tired of fighting to be valued. Tired of fighting to be seen. Tired of fighting to be supported. Begging people to stand with me. I am alone, and I am exhausted. This is fucking exhausting.

(A moment.)

RASHAD. I feel so stupid... I've said I love you but how could I... I'm sorry I failed you... I see it now... I see you – I value you – And Gen, I believe you. And I wanna be there, not as your man, but because you deserve it.

(A moment. **GENESIS** *doesn't respond.)*

(A moment.)

It's okay. I'mma give you the space you asked for. But know I'm here, if you need me.

(He begins gathering his things.)

(A moment. He is about to leave.)

GENESIS. Rashad...

(He swiftly throws his things down and immediately goes to her. A moment.)

(She finally turns to face him.)

(They look at each other. They have said all they could say.)

(Blackout.)

End of Play

CPSIA information can be obtained
at www.ICGtesting.com
Printed in the USA
BVHW032252161122
652180BV00011B/154

9 780573 708350